EMOTIMANIA

Do you love all things emoti?
Then this activity book is perfect for you!
Inside you will find:

Fun activity pages, cool emoti puffy
stickers and cute, emoti press-outs
to display or give away!

How to use your press-out pieces:

BRILLIANT BOOKMARKS

Press out and decorate the bookmarks.

1 Pull out the card pages at
the back of the book.

2 Gently push the shapes
until they pop out.

3 Complete the press-out
pieces using doodles, colour
and your puffy stickers.

*make
believe
ideas*

EMOTI DICTIONARY

Use colour to finish the emotis.

 angelic

 bear

 best friends

 birthday

 bow

 bowling

 bun

 butterfly

 cactus

 camera

 celebration

 chick

 cool

 cr

 cycling

 dancing

 days out

 diamond

 dizzy

 dolphin

 eat

 elephant

 excited

 family

 fish

 flamingo

 flattered

flo

 friends

 frog

 games

 gaming

 geeky

 good

gran

 grandpa

 guitar

 hair flick

 happy

 heart

 kisses

  kitt

 koala

 ladybird

 lightning

 lion

 lipstick

 love

make

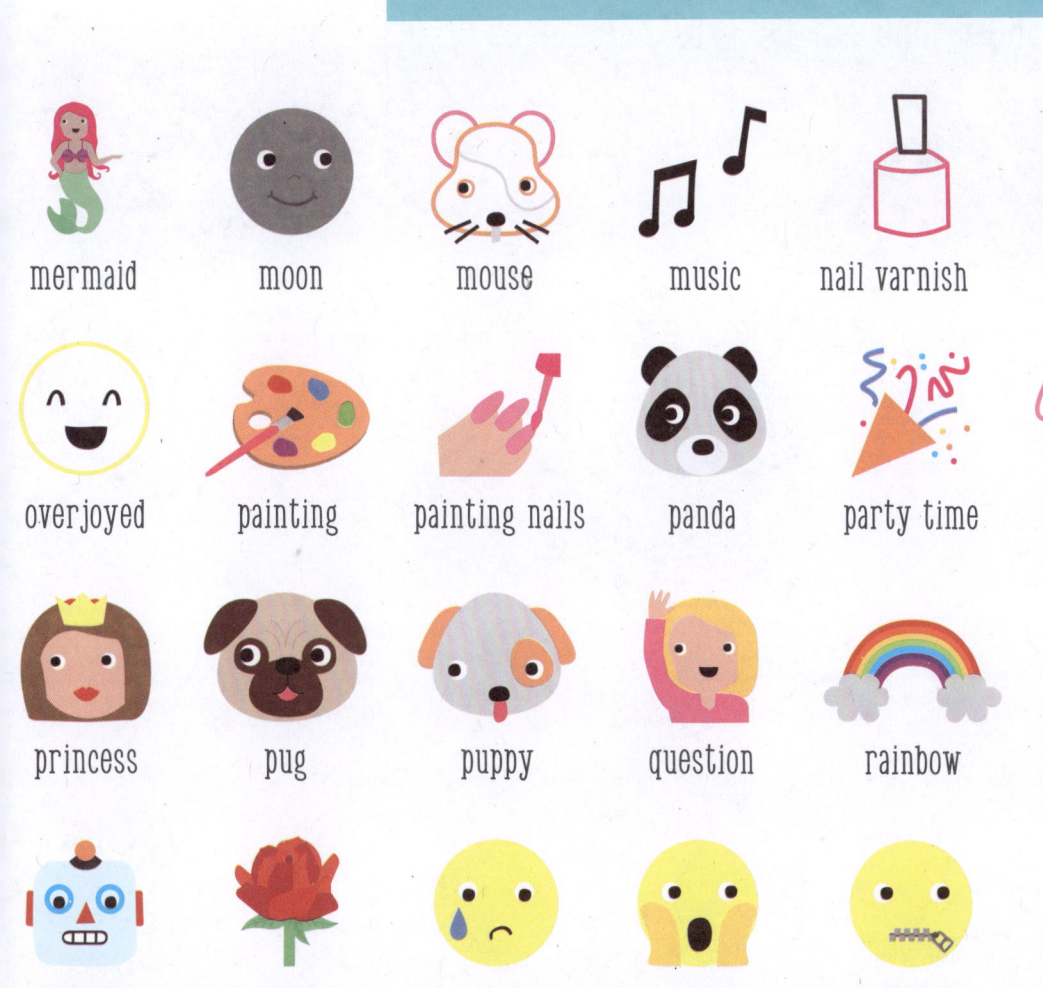

mermaid	moon	mouse	music	nail varnish	no deal	octopus
overjoyed	painting	painting nails	panda	party time	pig	playing music
princess	pug	puppy	question	rainbow	raining	reading
robot	rose	sad	scared	secret	shocked	shoe shopping

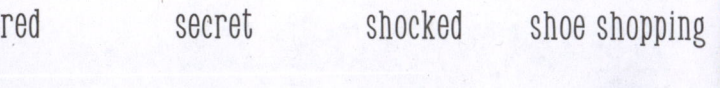

silly	singing	sleepy	snake	snowing	special occasion	sports
star	storm	strong	sunglasses	sunny	television	tennis

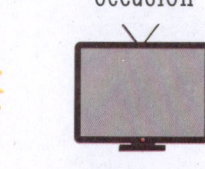

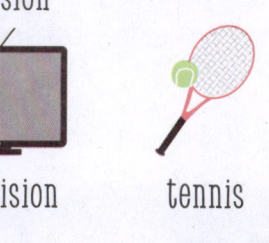

thank you	tiger	travelling	turtle	umbrella	unicorn	whale

MY FRIENDS

In the frames, draw your friends as emotis.

Write your friend's name here.

MERMAID MAZE

Use the key to help the mermaid through the maze.

  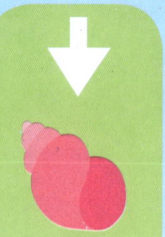 

Start

Finish

6

SUMMER FUN

Find all eight emotis in the grid.
Words can go across, down or diagonally.

butterfly

dress

flowers

pineapple

sandals

shell

sun

sunglasses

```
p i n e a p p l e s
s u n v b t d r e a
f r d e s h e l l n
l g e r e a t b a d
o w c s e l s e r a
w u e r s s s l k l
e c a l o m s t c s
r b u t t e r f l y
s u n g l a s s e s
```

Decorate the butterflies
and colour the flowers.

EMOTI NAILS

Design amazing emoti nail art.

Doodle some more emoti bracelets and rings.

PUTTING ON A SHOW

Can you help the singer find her lost microphone?

Start

Finish

Finish the audience emotis:

EMOTI HAPPY

Design your own emotis for the things that make you smile!

PEOPLE

FOOD

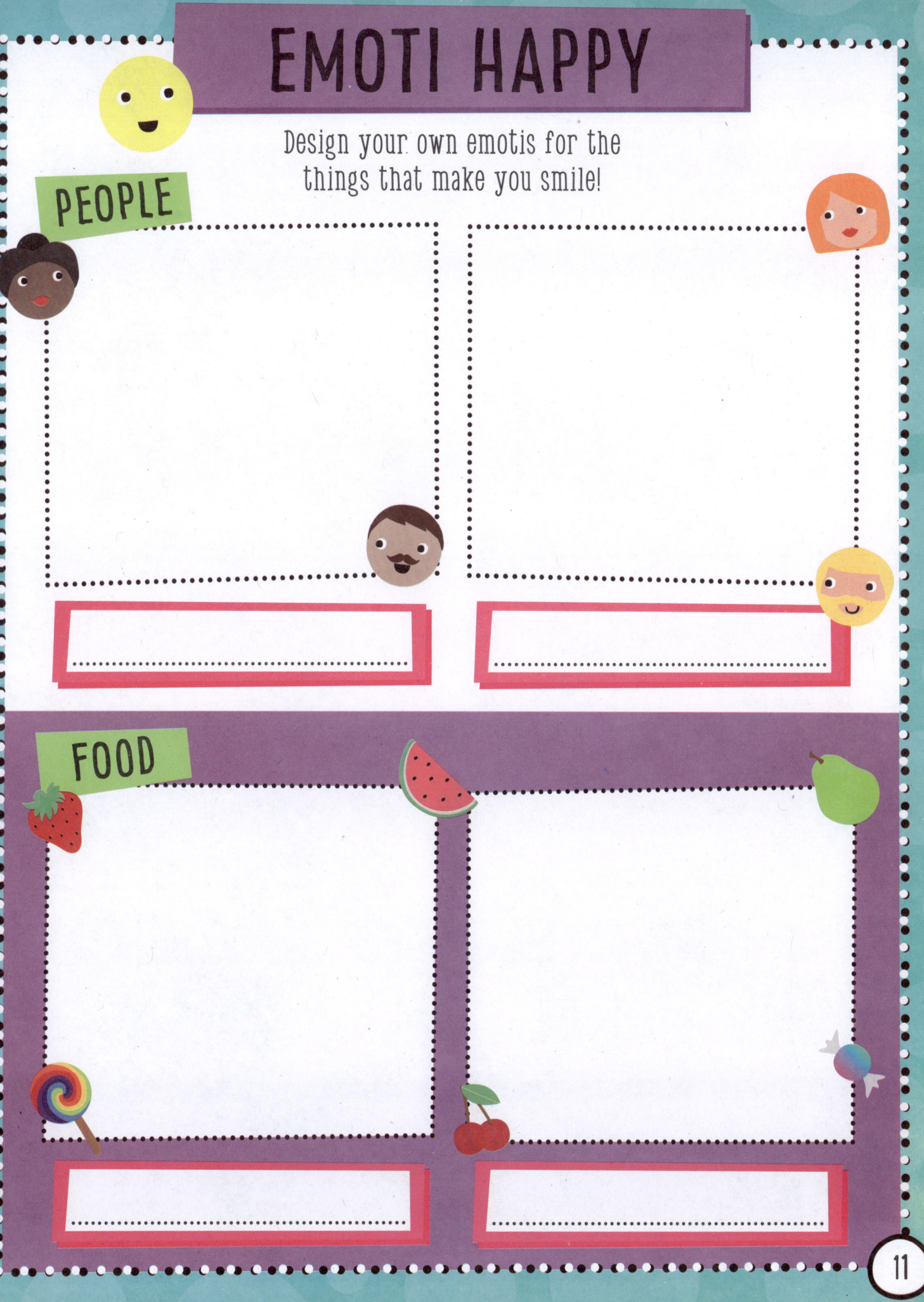

EMOTI-SHIRT

Draw and doodle cool emoti designs on the T-shirts.

CUTE CUPCAKES

Colour and decorate the emoti cupcakes.

MONKEY MADNESS

Which monkey is the odd one out?

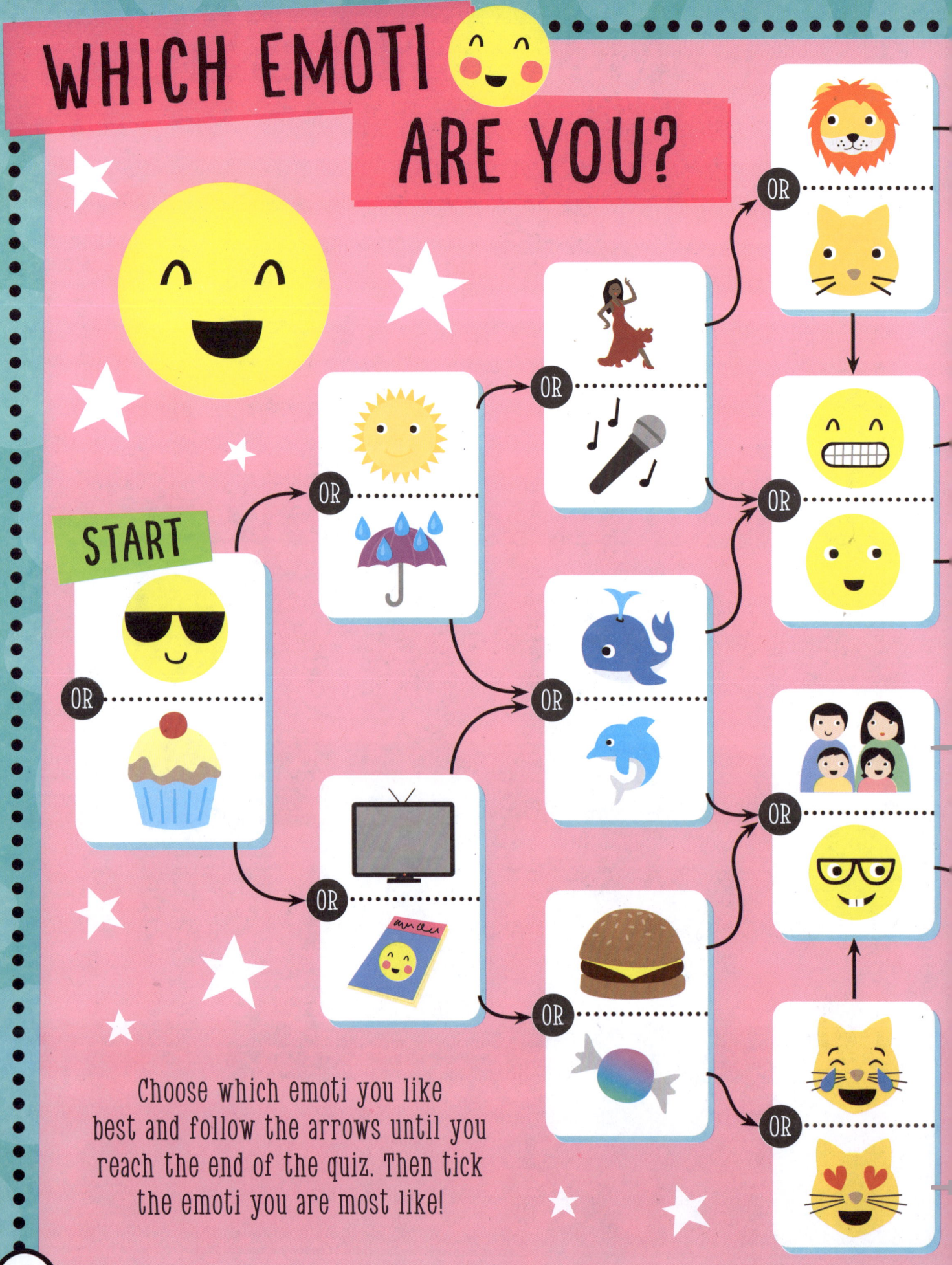

WHICH EMOTI ARE YOU?

START

Choose which emoti you like best and follow the arrows until you reach the end of the quiz. Then tick the emoti you are most like!

SWEET COOKIE

Your friends and family love you because you are so sweet and thoughtful.

PARTY SHOE

You are the life and soul of any party and love dancing and having fun.

CUTE PUPPY

You love animals and are very good at cheering people up when they are feeling upset.

DOODLE TIME

Doodle emoti faces in the yellow circles.

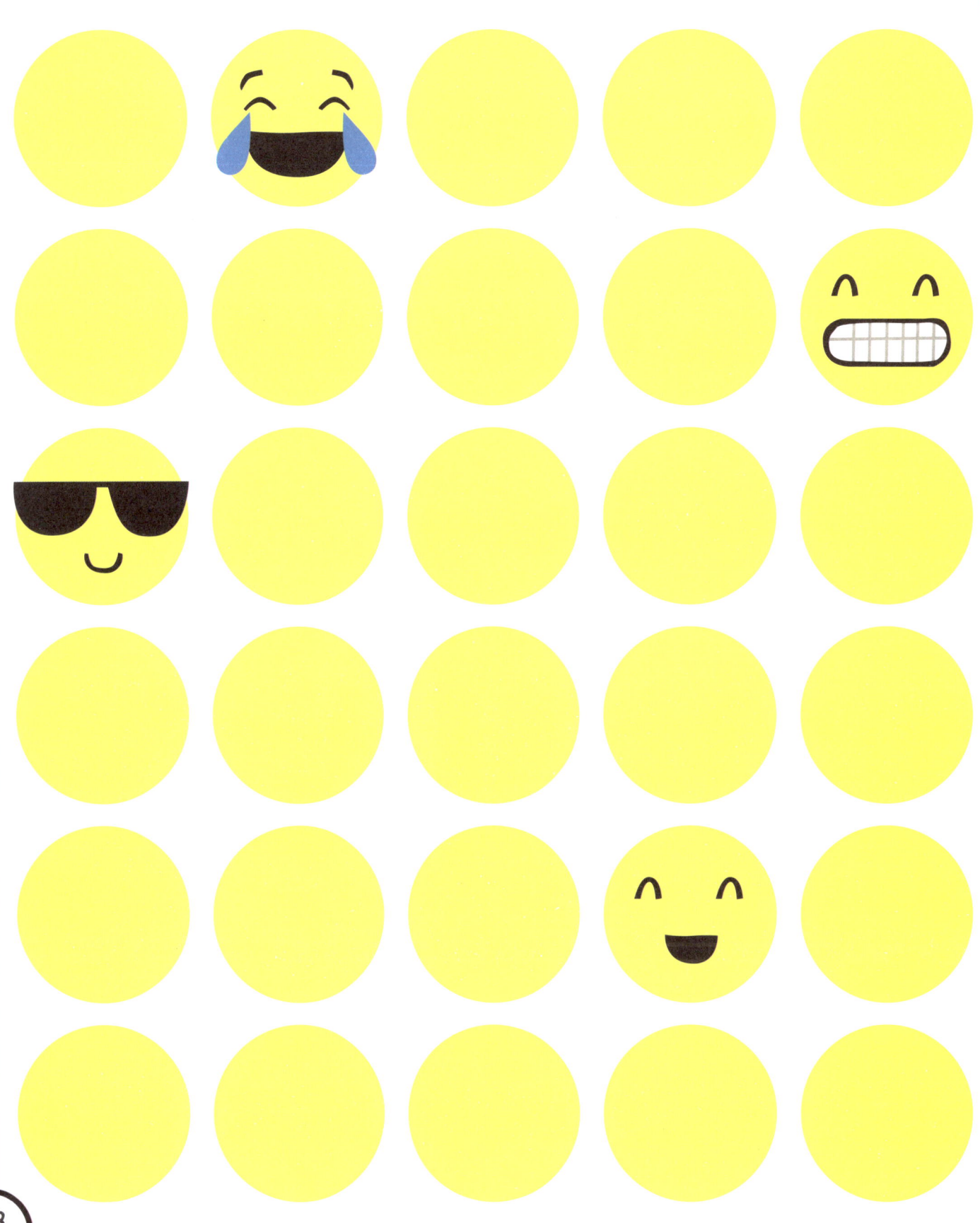

EMOTI ART

Copy the emotis. Use the grids to help you.

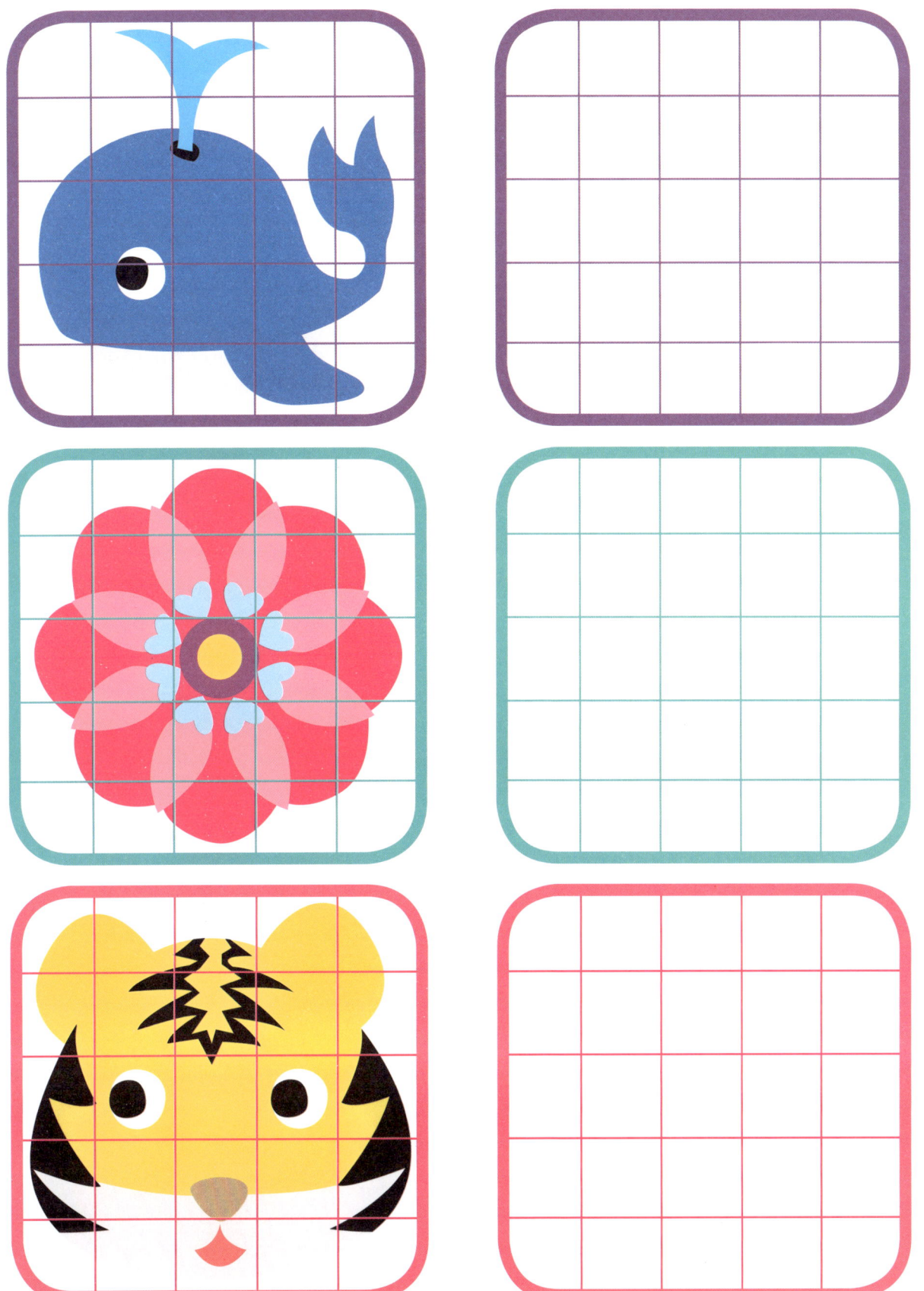

MY FAMILY

In the frames, draw members of your family as emotis.

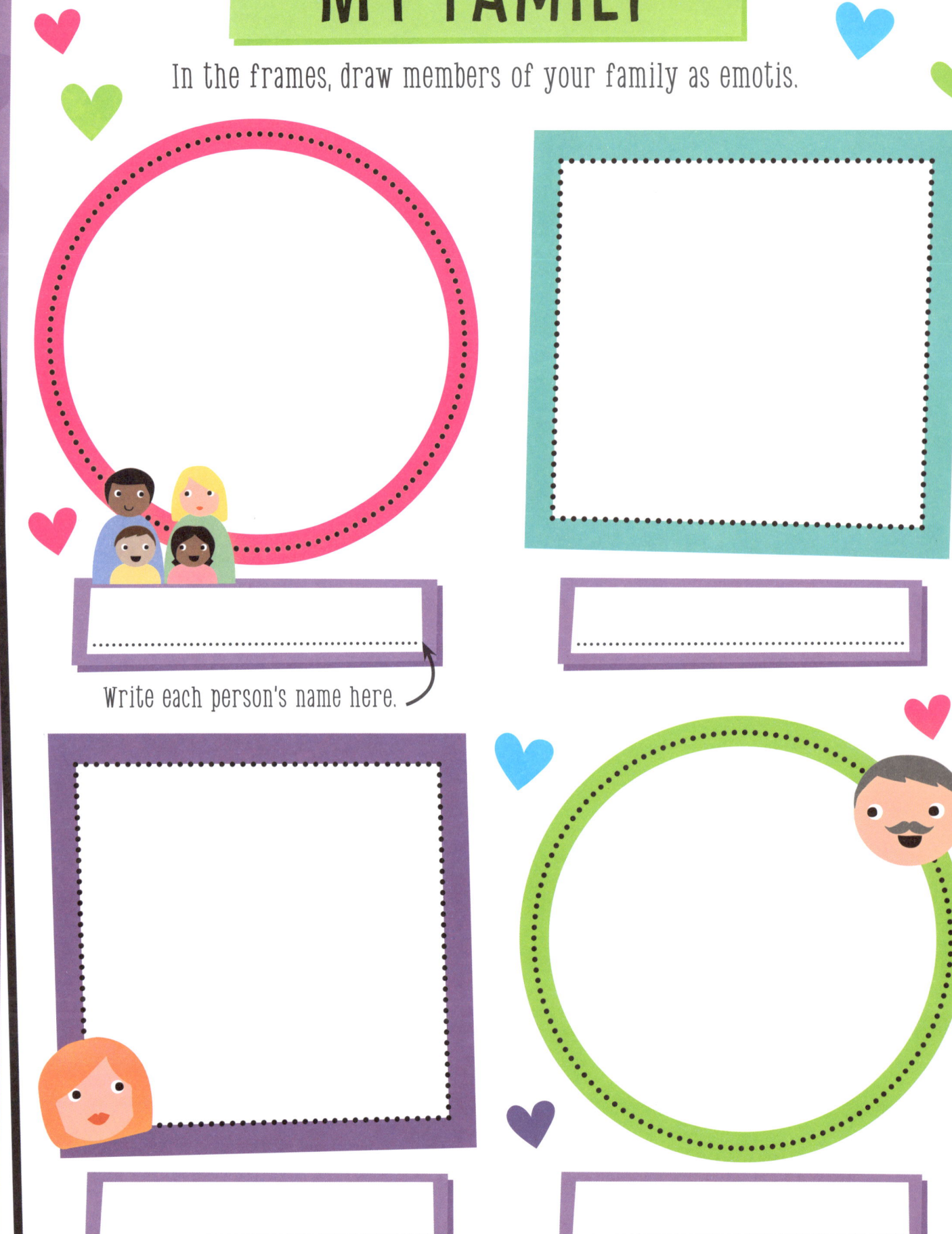

Write each person's name here.

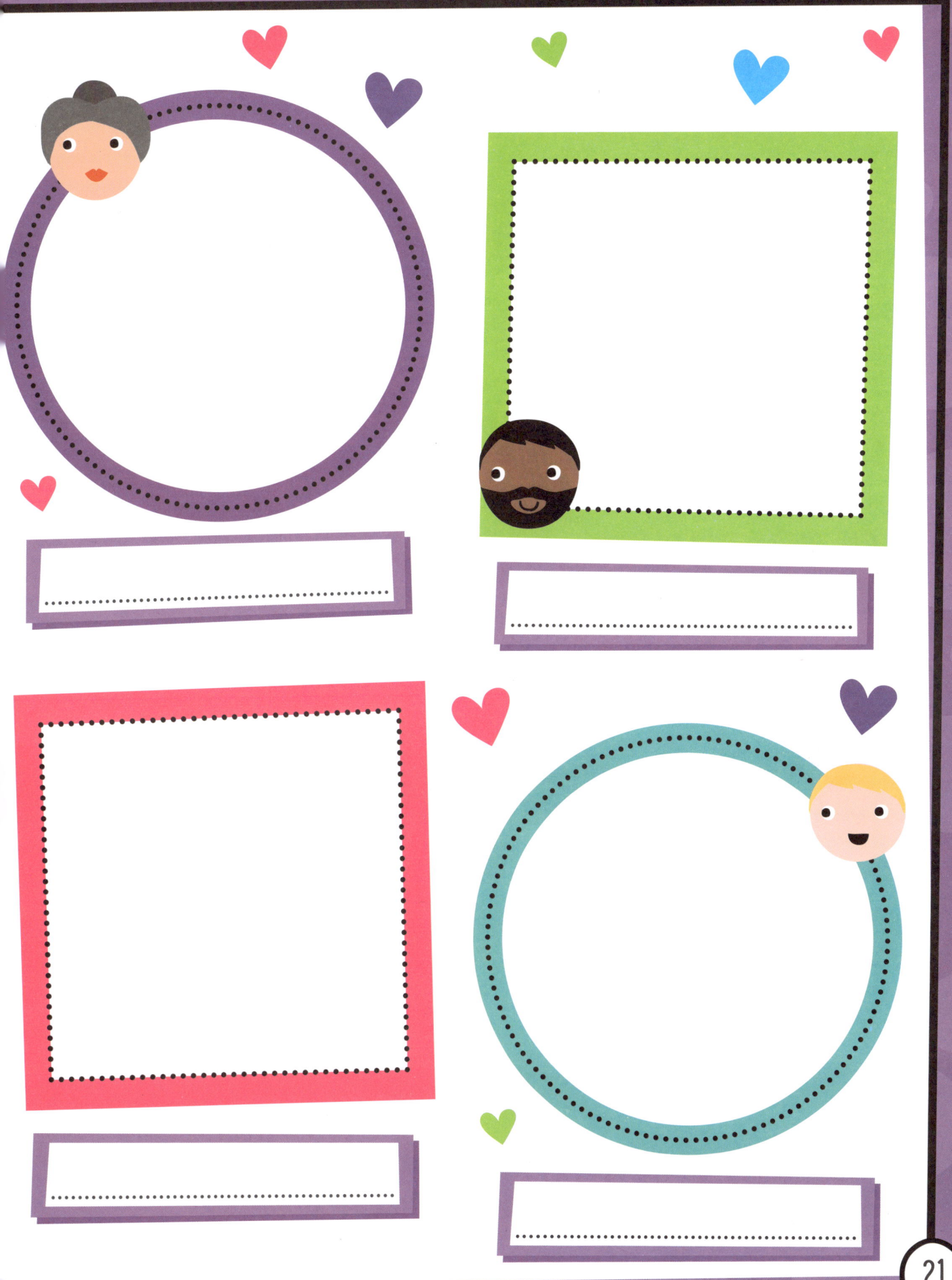

21

WHAT'S IN MY BAG?

Doodle three emotis for the things you
would need if you were going to . . .

A SLEEPOVER

SCHOOL

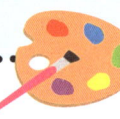

THE BEACH

COMPLETE THE CIRCLE

Fill the circle with more emoti faces.

Try to include
these emotis:

MY EMOTI SLEEPOVER

Design emoti pyjamas for you and your friends
to wear at your emoti sleepover!

Colour the sleepover activities, and then circle your top three.

Colour the midnight snacks, and then circle your top three.

Doodle emotis on your overnight bag.

WINTER WISHES

Find all eight emotis in the grid.
Words can go across, down or diagonally.

coat

hat

igloo

mittens

penguin

scarf

snowflake

snowman

s	n	o	w	f	l	a	k	e	s
n	c	n	v	b	t	d	r	e	a
o	r	a	e	s	h	e	p	l	i
w	g	e	r	e	a	t	e	a	g
m	w	h	s	f	l	s	n	r	l
a	u	e	a	s	s	s	g	k	o
n	c	o	a	t	m	s	u	c	o
r	q	o	v	f	b	r	i	l	y
s	u	m	i	t	t	e	n	s	s

Finish the scarf, hat and mittens with emoti designs.

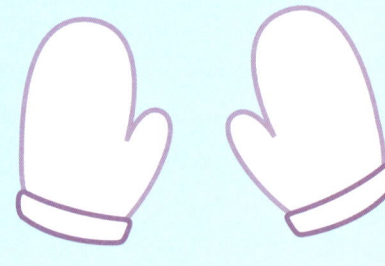

Rearrange the letters to
make a winter word.

RSAFC

....

DANCING QUEEN

Use the key to help the dancer through the maze!

↑	→	↓	←
👠	💎	⭐	👗

Start

Finish

1ST

EMOTI PAIRS

Draw lines to join the pairs of emotis. Can you join them without any of your lines crossing each other?

MAGICAL UNICORNS

Complete the unicorns using rainbow colours.

EMOTI FUN

Design your own emotis for the things
that you think are really fun!

ACTIVITIES

PLACES

KITTEN CRAZY

Which kitten is the odd one out?

Press out and decorate the door hanger.

KEEP OUT!

JUST TO SAY . . .

Press out and complete the card,
and then give it to a friend.

POSTCARDS

Press out and complete the postcards,
and then give them to your friends.

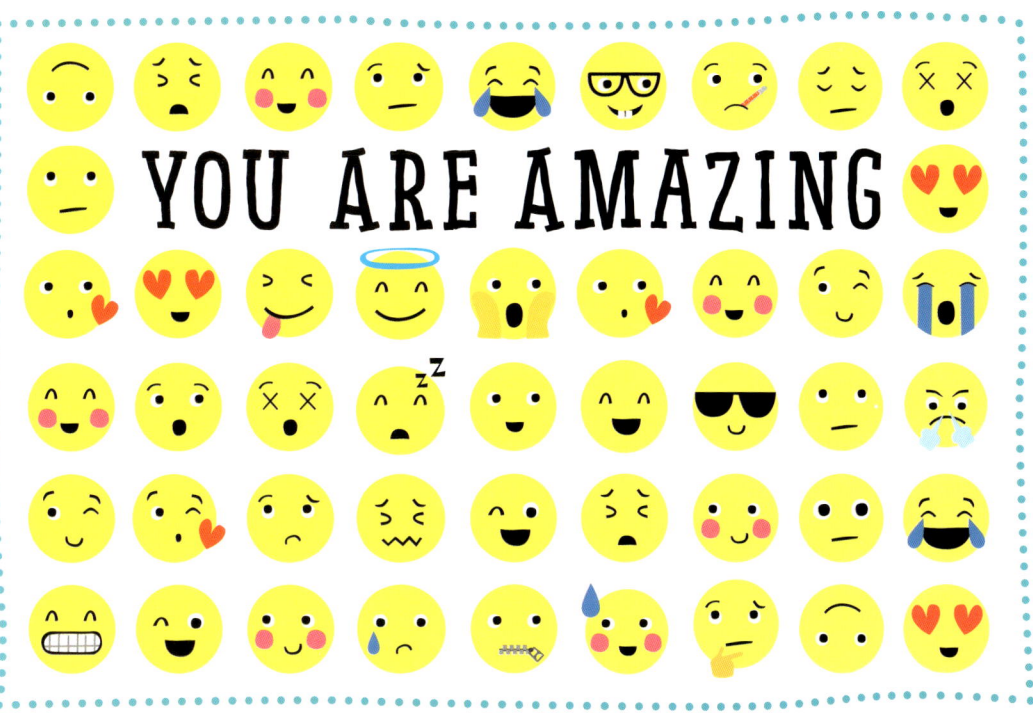

YOU ARE AMAZING

SO CUTE

BRILLIANT BOOKMARKS

Press out and decorate the bookmarks.

EMOTI FLAGS

Press out each flag and fold the tops
over some ribbon. Tape them down at the back,
and then hang them wherever you want!

Press out
and decorate
the door hanger.

Glam zone!

JUST TO SAY . . .

Press out and complete the card,
and then give it to a friend.

POSTCARDS

Press out and complete the postcards,
and then give them to your friends.

JUST TO SAY . . .

BRILLIANT BOOKMARKS

Press out and decorate the bookmarks.